MW00964426

Mia, Matt and the Lazy Gator

Annie Langlois

Illustrated by Jimmy Beaulieu
Translated by Sarah Cummins

Formac Publishing Company Limited
Halifax

Originally published as *Sculpture de Nestor l'alligator*
Copyright © 2007 Les éditions de la courte échelle inc.
Translation Copyright © 2010 Sarah Cummins
First Published in the United States in 2011.

Formac Publishing Company Limited acknowledges the support of the
province of Nova Scotia through the Department of Tourism, Culture and
Heritage. We acknowledge the financial support of the Government of Canada
through the Canada Book Fund for our publishing activities. We acknowledge
the support of the Canada Council for the Arts for our publishing program.

NOVA SCOTIA
Tourism, Culture and Heritage

The Canada Council | Le Conseil des Arts
for the Arts | du Canada

Canadä

Library and Archives Canada Cataloguing in Publication

Langlois, Annie, 1975-
[Sculpture de Nestor l'alligator. English]

     Mia, Matt and the lazy gator / Annie Langlois ; illustrator, Jimmy
Beaulieu ; translator, Sarah Cummins.

Translation of: La sculpture de Nestor l'alligator.
Issued also in an electronic format.

ISBN 978-0-88780-938-5 (bound).—ISBN 978-0-88780-936-1 (pbk.)
     1. Alligators—Juvenile fiction. I. Beaulieu, Jimmy, 1974-
II. Cummins, Sarah III. Title. IV. Title: Sculpture de Nestor
l'alligator. English.

PS8573.A5645S2813 2010   jC843'.6   C2010-902667-5

Formac Publishing Company Limited
5502 Atlantic Street
Halifax, NS,
Canada B3H 1G4
www.formac.ca

Distributed in the United States by:
Orca Book Publishers
P.O. Box 468
Custer, WA U.S.A.
98240-0468

Printed and bound in Canada
Manufactured by Transcontinental Métrolitho in Sherbrooke, Quebec, Canada
in August 2010.
Job # 23274

FSC

Mixed Sources
Cert no. SW-COC-000952
© 1996 FSC

Table of Contents

1

Do Alligators Bite?

Already it was almost time to leave for Blackfly Lake. For once, the time had flown by. I was busy with my final tests and my job as director of the year-end festival at school.

My brother Matt had choreographed a hip-hop dance for the show. His group was a big hit. Matt had a posse of girls

following him around, including Eloise, my best friend.

From my bedroom I could hear Uncle Orlando singing. He was delighted to be moving back to the country for the summer, knowing he'd be with his charming sweetheart, Maria.

Finally I was ready to go, but Matt was still talking on the phone. I listened at the door. Hmmm, he was talking to Eloise.

"Sure, you can call me at the cottage. Didn't Mia give you the number?"

I hadn't even thought of giving her the number, so I felt a bit guilty. But on the other hand, she never asked me for it!

I opened the door a crack to spy on Matt. I don't know what Eloise said to him, but he suddenly blushed, stammered and hung up.

I walked in, pretending I had just got there.

"Time to get ready, Mr. Popularity!"

Matt wasn't listening. He didn't even know I was there. He walked over to the closet and pulled out his suitcase. In three minutes and forty-five seconds, he was packed and ready to go.

When we got into the back seat of the car, he still hadn't opened his mouth.

"Are you all right, Matt?" asked Orlando.

"What? Yeah…"

Orlando and I were not so sure, but we let it drop. Matt was definitely in some other zone. He wasn't himself. What had Eloise done to him?

By the time we got to the cottage, Matt was more or less back to normal. We were both eager to find out what animal we would be spending time with this summer.

Uncle Orlando is a top animal wrangler for television and movies. Every summer, a new animal has a starring role in our summer vacation!

Matt and I raced to the barn, trying to guess what we would find there.

"I bet it's a gazelle!" I gasped as I galloped.

"No! A lion!" roared Matt, running along beside me.

We opened the massive wooden doors to the barn. Surprise! It was empty. Total silence reigned.

Disappointed, we trudged back to the car. Orlando had a mischievous look on his face.

"This year, kids," he announced, "we're raising the animals at a different location."

"Where?" demanded Matt.

Orlando nodded in the direction of the pond.

"I know! I know!" cried Matt.

Then he started hopping around, yelling "Ribbit! Ribbit!"

Orlando managed to keep a straight face as he shook his head no. We all headed over to the pond. I prayed we wouldn't be raising leeches.

Matt totally flipped out when he saw the strange and enormous beast.

"Wow! An alligator!"

I was not so excited. An alligator? What could you train an alligator to do? And I wondered ... do alligators bite?

2

Alligators Sleep

Matt's excitement soon faded. We'd been at the lake for three days and Gabe, our alligator, had moved all of seven centimetres.

This was a disaster for Orlando, who was supposed to train the gator to dance in an ad for an energy drink. The slogan was "Vita-Juice makes you want to dance!"

It was quite a challenge — teach one of the slowest, laziest animals on the planet to boogie. I had a feeling Orlando was going to need our help again!

"Gabe! Come here, Gabe!" Orlando coaxed.

Nothing doing. Orlando was not discouraged.

"It's only his first day of work," he said. "We have to be patient."

The gator basked in the sun, yawning from time to time. It looked like we were not going to have a very exciting summer.

We all started to yawn like Gabe. Then Orlando slipped away. It was time for him to go see Maria.

As soon as he left, something finally happened: Gabe moved!

He waddled over to a big mound of dirt mixed with twigs and leaves. He began patting it with his tiny paws.

I watched Gabe go back and forth between the pond and the mound. He seemed very serious and deliberate. After a moment, he backed up to check his work. He wasn't satisfied and set to work again, patting and smoothing the mound tirelessly.

"It looks like he's making a sculpture," I said.

Matt came over to check it out. Tact is not Matt's strong suit and he burst out laughing.

"I can't say it's a work of art, my friend!"

Gabe must have been miffed by this remark, because he nipped Matt on the bum. Not too hard, but enough to make Matt run off at top speed.

"Gabe, are you a sensitive soul, by any chance?" I asked.

He looked at me and snapped his jaws. I could tell that our artist needed privacy and space to create his art. I left before he bit me too.

Orlando was in the garden, whispering sweet nothings in Maria's ear. She gave him a few smooches in return. Inside the house, all was quiet. There was no sign of my runaway brother. I went upstairs to put on my bathing suit for a swim.

As I came to the bedroom door, I heard a murmur from the other side. Once again, I eavesdropped.

"I think about you all the time, too."

....

"I miss you even more."

I couldn't believe it! Matt was declaring his love! No wonder he was hiding! He was in love with my best friend!

And then I felt sad. Eloise hadn't asked to speak to me. What has Matt got that I haven't got? How come my friend never

called me to say how much she missed me? I went back downstairs. I wanted to tell Orlando how I felt, but he was too busy spooning with Maria in the backyard.

Honestly, this love business is too much! Everybody here needed privacy … except me.

3

Charming a Gator

To cheer myself up and get away from the lovebirds, I decided to concentrate on Gabe the Gator.

I thought about it for a few days and finally came up with an idea. Since love was all around me, I decided I would create a Lady Gator costume. A few smooches for Gabe, and he would be putty in my hands.

Everybody is a little silly when they're in love. We would be able to make him do whatever we wanted.

As I was finishing my handiwork, Matt strolled up.

"Wow!" he exclaimed. "What is that?"

I explained my plan. As usual, Matt was not very enthusiastic. I paraded around clacking the alligator jaws, but he still seemed sceptical.

"Mia, if Gabe bit me just because I teased him, he'll make mincemeat of you in that ridiculous costume."

"We'll see. In any case, you'll be wearing the costume."

He said that wasn't fair and so on and so forth. I paid no attention. He had done absolutely no work since the beginning of our vacation. I didn't feel the least bit sorry for him.

I went down to the pond to see Gabe. I had Orlando's camera in my pocket. If Matt thought he could steal Eloise from me, he had another think coming. I had my own idea about that.

Gabe was busy playing with his mound of dirt and paid no attention to me. He seemed to be in a hurry to finish his sculpture.

Matt joined me, wearing the alligator costume.

"Grrr," he growled, to let me know what a bad mood he was in. I didn't care.

"You need to get down on all fours, Matt. Like a real reptile."

"Mia!" he complained. "That's too much!"

"Shh! Alligators don't talk."

Matt lay on the ground and tried to crawl over to Gabe.

"Try to look pretty! You are trying to attract Gabe."

So Matt began to wriggle and writhe and make soft, sultry growling noises. He did whatever I told him. My revenge was sweet.

It was a scene worth saving for posterity. I discreetly snapped a few photos of my dorky brother, planning to show them to Eloise.

Soon the great flirtation turned to disaster. Gabe was not attracted to the fake lady alligator and began to roar madly.

"Brrrrruggghhh!"

It sounded like a deafening kind of

burp. Matt froze. Fortunately, Gabe turned away and crawled to the top of his gigantic mound.

"I think your costume needs a little more work, Mia," Matt mocked me.

All right, I'd have to think of another idea. But no way was I giving up so easily. Not on your life.

4

Come on, Gabe!

Gabe sulked for two weeks after that. He hardly budged from his mound of mud.

He would glare at us balefully whenever we approached, afraid we would send a fake lady alligator after him again. It offended his artistic soul.

Uncle Orlando was tearing his hair out with frustration. He tried to persuade

Vita-Juice to change their mascot, but in vain. They insisted on a dancing alligator.

Matt was not much help. He spent all his time sneaking away to call Eloise. Even when he was with us, his mind was elsewhere. It is really boring when your brother is in love.

But I didn't give up. I hung out at the pond, keeping Gabe company. I talked to him, explaining the situation and just chatting about this and that.

In any case, with Matt lost in love, there wasn't much else to do. I figured that if I was patient, something would come of it.

"Come on, Gabe. Give it a try!"

This time, I dared to approach him. I held my hand out to him, like you do with a dog.

"Gently, Gabe. Gently."

Luckily for me, Gabe didn't mind when I slipped my hand under his damp snout and petted him, while singing a little crocodile song.

"Crocodile on the Nile basking in the sun. Crocodile from the Nile wants to have some fun!"

Maybe the song reminded Gabe of happier times. He nodded his head in time. "Good Gabe! Good gator!"

I wanted to show someone. But there was no one around. No brother, no uncle, no neighbour. Just my luck. I kept on singing, while Gabe fluttered his feet.

A few minutes later, he was swinging his head back and forth. He looked like a hip-hop singer at his mic. I was so proud!

"All you needed, Gabe, was a coach!"

Bursting with pride, I ran off to announce the news to the others.

★★★

Matt and Maria were sitting on the porch swing. She was helping him write a love letter to Eloise. Phooey! What a waste of time.

"I know what you're going to say," I announced. "You'll say, 'Mia, you are the best!'"

"Now what?" sighed Matt.

"I have taught Gabe how to dance! Applause, please."

"No way!" Matt replied.

"Proof, Mia. I need proof," insisted Orlando, coming out of the house.

We all went down to the pond, where we found Gabe sound asleep. He must have been exhausted by our training session.

"Gabe," I called softly. "Please, wake up and show them what you can do."

Even though I was a bit embarrassed in front of them all, I began singing my song. The three of them just gaped at me. I guess they were surprised at my musical selection.

"Do you really think that song is going to make an alligator want to dance?" sneered Matt. "You're nuts!"

Gabe snoozed on. Was he doing it on purpose? I sang louder, hoping he would

wake up. But it just made the other three laugh harder. Even Maria was hooting.

I was mortified. But even I had to admit it was kind of funny.

5

Triumph

Afterwards, they never stopped kidding me and teasing me about my song.

I got fed up with it! I was the only one who was even trying to find a way to train that alligator! The others were just mooning around. Kissy-face, sweetie-pie, all the time! Get serious!

So I spent most of my time down by

the pond. I pretended to be watching the frogs, but in fact I was spying on Gabe.

One day I sensed that he was not feeling great. He seemed nervous. He climbed on his mound, then climbed back down. He waddled over to me and nudged me with his snout. Then he went back on the mound.

"What is it, Gabe?"

Gabe swung his long head up and down. As I walked over to the mound, I heard a strange sound. A sort of sharp squealing noise.

The squeals were coming from inside the mound. Gabe began to scratch at it impatiently. I figured he was asking for help.

"I'll help. Just wait a sec!"

The mud had dried in the sun into hard, solid walls. I needed reinforcements.

"Matt! Come here! Quick!"

Matt appeared in a flash, with Maria and Orlando running after him. Now there were four humans and one alligator scratching away at the huge pile of dried mud. Soon I had dirt under my nails and my hands were filthy.

"Grrrigrrrigrrri! Grrrigrrrigrrri! Grrrigrrrigrrri! Grrrigrrrigrrri!"

The squeals sounded louder and more frantic. But we had managed to open a crack in the wall. Then we worked to make it wider.

"Oh!" cried Maria. "Aren't they cute?"

She was the first one to figure out that we had hatched Gabe's babies.

"Gabe is a mother?" Matt said wonderingly, still dizzy from all his hard work.

"The little trickster!" cried Orlando, stunned.

I think he felt guilty that he hadn't been able to tell whether his alligator was female or male. Maybe he finally realized

he hadn't paid much attention to his work, what with Maria and her sweet kisses.

While I was thinking about all the time Orlando had wasted, Matt was counting the babies.

"Wow! There are thirty-three baby Gabies!"

One by one, we took them out of the nest, under the watchful eye of Mother Gabe, who — wouldn't you know it — promptly fell asleep.

★★★

Later on, Maria invited us to a picnic to celebrate the new mother and her babies.

We set up the picnic table near the pond, so we could watch the baby

alligators. Raising his glass of nasturtium juice, Orlando declared, "Mia, I have to congratulate you. Because of you, we were able to save these little chicks."

"They're called hatchlings," Matt corrected him.

"That's right. But thank you for sticking to it, Mia. You never gave up."

Then we raised our glasses and toasted me. It was about time they recognized my hard work and patience!

We looked on the internet and found out that the mound was the nest where Gabe had laid her eggs. And here I thought she was an artist making her sculpture! How wrong can you be?

At my feet, two little alligators nibbled on my shoelaces. I slipped them a piece of the blueberry crumble Maria had made. They greedily gobbled it up.

That gave me an idea. I would need Matt's help again. But it would have to wait until the next day.

6

Gator Hip-Hop

It was just after five o'clock the next morning when I woke up Matt.

"Hurry, Matt! Get up! We've got something to do."

He stretched, yawned, rolled over and fell back asleep. It was time to try Plan B.

"Matt, Eloise is on the phone for you."

He was up in seven seconds flat. When

he realized I had tricked him, he was not happy.

"Matt, I promise you it will be lots of fun. Come on, hurry!"

Before leaving the house, I picked up my MP3 player and the speakers from Orlando's computer.

The baby alligators were not as lazy as Matt. They were already awake and playing in the pond. I called their mom over and explained our plan.

"Gabe, we have to help Orlando keep his reputation as the top trainer. Can we count on your help?"

Gabe was happy to help. She called her babies into a half-circle around her. I decided I would be the emcee. "Friends, today you will have the chance to become

stars of the small screen. May I introduce you to your coach — Kool Man Matt!"

As the hip-hop music blasted out, Matt jumped up and started his routine from the end-of-school fest.

The baby alligators loved it. And what about Gabe? She seemed to have caught the same bug as Eloise. The mama alligator seemed to have fallen under Matt's spell — finally!

★★★

After rehearsing for several hours, the alligators hadn't quite got their dance down, but they were nearly there. We worked them very hard. Matt taught them the steps, while I handled the staging.

Our teamwork was brilliant! By the end of the afternoon, we were ready to put on the show. Orlando couldn't believe it.

"What would I do without you two treasures?" he asked, a tear in his eye.

Then he gave us the biggest hug ever. Matt was a bit embarrassed, in front of his new fans. He wriggled free, trying to look cool.

"So long, guys! See you tomorrow!" he called to the baby alligators.

As for me, I had been deprived of attention for so long that I was happy for all the hugs I could get!

7

Matt Rules!

When the evenings got too cool for us to eat dinner outside, we knew that was a sign that summer was nearly over.

The alligators would soon go to their owners in Florida. And we'd head back to the city. But for now, we were having a party in the barn!

The managers at Vita-Juice were

delighted! They had hoped for a dancing alligator, and they got thirty-four for the price of one! Their ad would air in the fall. We couldn't wait to see our little friends on TV.

Maria had cooked up a feast for our last evening with the alligator family. There was a daisy and beet soufflé for us and cricket fritters for the alligators.

Orlando had invited some of our friends to the party ... including Eloise.

The barn was filled with music and people were dancing. Matt was running back and forth between Eloise and Gabe. There was a bit of jealousy in the air. But still, we had a lot of fun!

"Your brother is really the greatest!" Eloise stopped dancing and stood next

to me. She gazed adoringly at Matt, who puffed out his chest to look like he had some muscles.

"Do you think he's still interested in me?" Eloise asked.

Now was the time to show her those photos of Matt disguised as a she-gator. I had thought that would be a laugh, but now I realized I was just jealous because my brother and my best friend were paying more attention to each other than to me. I put the camera away.

"He hasn't stopped mooning about you all summer long!" I whispered to Eloise.

She was so happy! She kissed me on the cheek and said the nicest thing.

"Mia, my best friend, I adore you!"

Then she went back to dance with

Matt. I looked at them whirling and laughing and I thought to myself, that's life. Matt won't always be there for me to have fun with. Neither will Eloise.

One thing wouldn't change, I consoled myself. Every summer, there would still be Orlando's animals, so I would never be bored or lonely. And one day I would meet my own Prince Charming. But I'm in no hurry.

More novels in the First Novels series!

Music by Morgan

Ted Staunton

Illustrated by Bill Slavin

Morgan has to get creative, and sneaky, if he wants to play music instead of floor hockey. He crafts a plan to swap places with Aldeen — but how long will they pull it off before they get caught?

Raffi's New Friend

Sylvain Meunier

Illustrated by Élisabeth Eudes-Pascal

Translated by Sarah Cummins

Raffi and the new girl in school, Fatima, have something in common: neither of them quite fit in. They bond when they find they have something else in common: a love of birds.

Daredevil Morgan

Ted Staunton

Illustrated by Bill Slavin

Will Morgan be brave enough to try the GraviTwirl ride at the Fall Fair? Can he win the "Best Pumpkin Pie" contest, or will Aldeen Hummel, the Godzilla of grade three, interfere?

Raffi's For the Birds

Sylvain Meunier

Illustrated by Élisabeth Eudes-Pascal

Translated by Sarah Cummins

Raffi wants to save the birds by protesting the destruction of the trees they nest in. While he may have trouble walking, he has lots of ideas, and friends ready to help!